Endangered Animals

by David Orme

Ransom

Trailblazers

Endangered Animals
by David Orme
Educational consultant: Helen Bird

Illustrated by Ed Tucker

Published by Ransom Publishing Ltd.
51 Southgate Street, Winchester, Hants. SO23 9EH
www.ransom.co.uk

ISBN   978 184167 691 3

First published in 2009

Copyright © 2009 Ransom Publishing Ltd.

Endangered Animals

$5-99

Contents

Get the facts   **5**

What's the problem?   6

What's happening?
  – Loss of habitat and climate change   8

  – Poaching and hunting   10

Case studies
  – Orangutans   12

  – Africa   14

Animals already extinct   16

Fiction

Where the Forest Ended   19

Endangered Animals word check   **36**

Endangered Animals

Get the facts

What's the problem?

Some scientists say there could be **two hundred million** different types of living things in the world.

Nobody really knows, because most of them haven't been found yet!

This animal is the **Borneo Clouded Leopard**. Until 2007, no one knew it was a different species from other leopards.

Some types of living things are in danger of becoming **extinct**.

Some have become extinct already.

Many will disappear before we even find them.

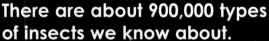

There are about **900,000 types of insects we know about.**

There could be millions more types waiting to be found.

6

Every year a list of animals in danger is made. This is called the red list.

Here are some of the animals on the red list.

Animal	The problem	Numbers
Bears (including polar bears, black and brown bears, and pandas)	Climate change. Poaching (parts of their bodies are used for medicine). Loss of forests.	In big trouble where they are not protected.
Black Rhinos	Killed for their horns.	1970 – 65,000. Now – Less than 3,000.
Blue Whale	Hunted until 1964. They have not managed to recover from this.	Early 20th century – about 200,000. Now – about 2,500.
Gorilla	War, loss of forests, disease.	About 100,000, but no one is sure. Some people think numbers are going up because of good conservation.
Great White Shark	Fishing.	No one knows – but the numbers are going down fast.

What's happening?

Loss of habitat and climate change

Our world is changing. *Why?*

❋ **There are more and more people in the world.**

They need places to live, and land to grow food. Areas like **rain forests** are **disappearing**. Trees are cut down for timber.

The land is planted with crops like these **oil palm trees**.

These places do not make a good habitat for wild animals.

Sometimes the rain forest is cut down to make room for **mines** for metal such as **gold** or **copper**.

This is the Kennecott copper mine, in Utah, USA.

Trail Blazers

 The climate is changing.

This is mainly because of the **greenhouse gases** we are putting into the air.

Any change in the climate will affect wild life.

Rain forests might get drier.

Some places could become deserts.

The sea will get warmer. This will seriously affect sea life.

9

What's happening?

(2) Poaching and hunting

Animals are killed for many reasons.

People may want them for **food**.

People think that parts of some animals make good **medicine**.

> Chimpanzees are eaten in Africa. (It is called bush meat.)

> Rhino horns are used in medicine (and, no, it doesn't work.)

The animals may kill farm animals or damage crops.

> Elephants can do a lot of damage to crops!

Some people just enjoy killing animals.

Fishing

A lot of our **food** comes from the sea. Fishing is a type of hunting. These creatures are **wild animals** that have to be caught.

(Well, not the fish fingers – but they *are* made from wild animals!)

So what's the problem?

If too many of these creatures are caught, there won't be enough left to breed and produce young ones. The **species** will **disappear**. This is already happening.

Some people love eating **cod** with their chips. But these fish are disappearing fast.

Other problems

Fishing can cause problems for other sea animals. The fish that are taken may be the food for other animals, such as dolphins or seabirds.

Case study – Orangutans

Where do they live?

Orangutans live in rainforests on the islands of Borneo and Sumatra.

Borneo

Sumatra

Why are they in danger?

They are losing their habitat because the rain forest is being cut down.

Are there any other dangers?

Orangutans are sometimes killed by poachers.

Sometimes they kill them because they damage crops.

 Sometimes the **mothers** are **killed** so the **babies** can be taken.

Some very silly people think orangutans make good **pets.**

How fast are they disappearing?

There are only about **25,000 animals** left in the wild. Ten years ago there were twice as many. If nothing is done, the animal will become **extinct** in the wild by about **2020**.

Is anything being done? Yes!

Nature reserves have been set up. These are guarded to protect the animals.

Organisations such as the **Sepilok Orangutan Appeal UK** do a lot of work to protect the animals.

Visit their website (***www.orangutan-appeal.org.uk***) to find out more.

Case study – Africa

Why does Africa have problems?

Population

There are now three times more people in Africa than there were fifty years ago. All these people need a place to live and to grow food.

Poverty

Many African countries are poor. They cannot afford to spend money on protecting wildlife. Hunting animals is a way for very poor people to make money.

War

Wars in Africa have had serious effects on wildlife.

Climate change

Drought in parts of Africa means that some places are turning into desert.

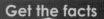
Trail Blazers

These African animals are in danger!

Black Rhinoceros

Cheetah

Pygmy hippopotamus

Leopard

Gorilla

You can help!

Visit www.panda.org to see how.

Nile crocodile

15

Animals already extinct

Many thousands of animals have already become extinct. Here are just a few of them.

Passenger Pigeon
(USA)
Last one died 1914

Golden Toad
(Costa Rica)
Last seen 1989

Quagga
(South Africa)
Last one died 1883

Auroch (Europe)

Last one killed in 1627

Arabian Ostrich (Arabian Peninsula)

Last one eaten about 1940

Tasmanian Wolf

Last one died around 1950

Dodo (Mauritius)

Last one died 1683

Where the Forest Ended

This is a true story.

There *was* an orangutan called Julie, and this *did* happen to her.

And this is a picture of the *actual* bus stop in Borneo where she was found (at the end of the story).

Chapter 1:
Julie's story

Life had been hard for Julie.

Poachers had taken her from her mother when she was a baby. The poachers had shot her mother.

Then she was sold. She was sent to a foreign country to be a pet.

Her new owners didn't understand how to look after wild animals.

When Julie grew up, she was hard to control.

Her owners didn't want her any more.

An animal rescue group tried to teach her how to live in the rain forest.

At first, Julie didn't know how to find food for herself.

She learnt by copying the older orangutans.

At last, the people who ran the centre decided she was ready for the wild.

She was taken back to the rain forest.

But she didn't like it!

Chapter 2:
Chain saws

The rain forest was a big place, full of strange sounds and smells.

Julie wanted to go back to where she had been looked after. She set off through the rain forest.

She had learnt from the other orangutans how to travel fast through the trees. There seemed no end to her journey.

At last, she reached a place where the forest ended.

Here, she heard a strange, new noise.

Julie had reached a clearing in the forest.

The sound she heard was chain saws. Men were busy cutting down the forest trees.

The forest had been cool, but here the hot sun burnt down.

The buzz of the chainsaws and the crash of the trees frightened the animal.

She slipped back into the forest.

Chapter 3:
The palm oil plantation

Days passed. Julie had managed to find some food, but not enough. She was hungry.

One evening she came to a place where all the trees were the same, and were set out in rows. They were oil palms.

Some of the trees were small. They had tender green shoots.

Julie tried them. They were good! She started eating.

She didn't see the man creeping up on her with a gun.

The man took aim and fired.

She came to a place where oil palms had been planted in rows.

But this place was dangerous ...

DACORUM LRC

Luckily for Julie, it was quite dark. She felt the bullet whistle past her head.

She did not understand what the sound was. But it stirred up a bad memory in her. She ran, not knowing where she was going.

Another shot. Another bullet flew by.

She ran back into the rainforest. She was safe.

Chapter 4:
The road

The next day, Julie found a road through the forest.

She had started to feel safe in the forest. Should she cross the road, or go back?

Then she heard a noise, getting louder and louder. It was a truck, heading up the road to a huge copper mine.

Another truck, full of people, came down from the mine.

Julie remembered the people who looked after her at the centre.

She started to walk down the road.

When a truck went by, she hid in the trees.

At last she reached some buildings. There was a bus stop there.

Julie waited at the stop until a bus came along.

The driver was very surprised! He called the centre.

'Right!' said the woman who picked them up. 'It's back to the forest for you!'

Endangered Animals word check

breed	oil palm
chain saw	orangutan
climate	poaching
conservation	population
drought	poverty
extinct	protected
greenhouse gases	rain forest
habitat	rescue
marshlands	species
nature reserves	wild life